Anna Finds a Friend

By
KATE EGAN

Illustrated By
ELISABETTA MELARANCI

Disney PRESS
Los Angeles • New York

For Maëlys

—K.E.

FAC-029261-20017
ISBN 978-1-368-05604-5

Printed in the United States of America
First Paperback Edition, March 2020
10 9 8 7 6 5 4 3 2 1

Book design by Maureen Mulligan

Visit disneybooks.com

Chapter 1
Goodbye and Hello

Anna looked out from the castle window. On the bridge far below, she could see a carriage crossing the bright blue water. King Agnarr and Queen Iduna, Anna's parents, were inside that carriage. They needed to take care of important business and would be gone for two weeks.

"We'll be back before you know it," her mother had said. She stroked her daughter's hair. "We will miss you while we are gone."

"I'll miss you, too," Anna had replied, giving her mother a long hug.

She blew kisses and waved at the carriage until it disappeared into the distance.

Anna was eight years old, and this was the first time her parents were traveling without her. She would miss having tea in the mornings with her mother, and reading stories in the afternoons with her father. She would do her lessons as usual, but life at the castle would be totally different.

But Anna had decided she was not going to let her parents' trip get her down! Anna would make her own fun.

After one last look out the window, Anna hurried down the spiral stairs and raced to her room. Miss Larsen, Anna and her sister Elsa's governess, had told Anna she could have some free time before lessons. It was the perfect day to play pretend, Anna decided. She took a sheet off her bed and circled it around herself. The long end trailed behind her like a train.

Anna bowed at herself in the mirror, pretending to be an elegant lady. She imagined the sheet was a beautiful party dress. "Charmed, I'm sure," she said to her reflection, twirling dramatically. Her new dress was so beautiful that she wanted to show everyone else in the castle.

She hurried into the hallway and stopped outside her older sister's bedroom door. Elsa never seemed to come out of her room now, at least not when Anna was around, but she'd loved making costumes before.

Anna knocked on Elsa's door. She adjusted the sheet and held the end of the train in her hand. "Elsa?" she said. "Wait till you see my new dress!"

But Elsa didn't open the door. "Go away, Anna," Elsa said.

Sighing, Anna continued down the hallway. She missed her sister, and the way things used to be. Not that long ago, the sisters had been close, and Arendelle Castle had bustled. Now the castle was closed to visitors, and Elsa had shut Anna out. Anna still didn't understand why everything had changed.

Anna swept grandly through the empty castle. She spun and leaped across the Great Hall, pretending she was at a ball. She took a short break from being fancy and slid across the smooth floor in her socks. Then she gathered up the train of her dress and continued to the kitchen.

"How do you like my dress?" Anna asked Olina, one of the castle workers, who was in the kitchen stirring something on the stove. Anna twirled before her. "Let's pretend we're going to a party!"

"I am just finishing this soup," said Olina, pointing at it with her spoon. "Why don't you come back a little later?"

When Anna left the kitchen, she found Kai and Gerda at the bottom of the stairs. They were polishing a suit of armor. They might not want to dress up, Anna thought, but maybe they could play a game.

"Count to ten, then try to find me!" Anna

said to the friendly housekeepers. Hide-and-seek was one of her favorites.

"We can play later," said Gerda. She was working on the knight's helmet. "Wait till you see him shine," she told Anna.

Anna did not want to wait, though.

She wished that "later" were *right now.*

Why didn't anyone want to play?

Luckily, she knew people who were always available. Anna skipped past Kai and Gerda and threw open the tall white doors that opened into the portrait gallery. It was a big room with a brilliant chandelier, and paintings lined the walls from floor to ceiling. Anna loved to imagine that the people in the paintings were real. They were always happy to see her!

"Good morning," she said to one of her favorites. She was a girl in a billowy green dress, riding high on a swing. "When can I teach you how to jump off that swing?"

Anna paused, as if the girl in the painting were really answering her. "Yes, yes, I know. But there's no reason to be nervous. I've done it lots of times!" She didn't know why the girl was worried.

Nearby, two more of Anna's "friends" were lying on a blanket in the woods, enjoying a picnic. "What's on the menu today?" Anna asked the pair. "Pancakes with chocolate chips? Those are my favorite!" She knew that people did not eat pancakes on *real* picnics. When she was pretending, though, anything was possible.

Anna daydreamed about going on a picnic with a real friend someday.

But if she couldn't go on a real picnic, Anna decided, she could at least eat real pancakes. At this time of day, she and her mother usually had tea and bread. No wonder she was getting hungry!

When Anna returned to the kitchen, Olina was tending the fire. Anna heard the pop and hiss of burning wood. She also heard an unusual sound at the kitchen's back door.

Was that the jingling of a carriage?

For a moment, Anna wondered if her parents had come back. She peeked outside hopefully, but she did not see a royal carriage. It was a smaller carriage, pulled by a single horse, with a pile of bundles in the back.

Anna had been dreaming of adventure, and an adventure had arrived! She couldn't remember the last time someone had come to the castle!

Someone would need to greet this visitor, Anna realized. Since Olina was distracted, she decided to take matters into her own hands.

Chapter 2
Castle Deliveries

The carriage driver smiled when he spotted Anna in the kitchen. "My name is Nikko," he said, tipping his hat. "I am here with the day's deliveries." He was tall and strong, with gray hair.

"The day's deliveries?" Anna asked. It sounded like he had been there before.

Olina turned from the fire to greet the carriage driver. "Nikko brings our supplies at this time every day," she explained to Anna. "Everything the castle could need or want."

Anna realized why she had never met him. He always came when she was having tea with her mom.

Curious, she looked at Nikko. "What do you do with the supplies?" she asked.

"I make my rounds inside the castle, dropping off whatever was ordered," he replied.

That sounded like an adventure to Anna. "Can I help?" she asked him.

"I would be honored to have you join me," said Nikko.

Anna put her sheet-dress aside and followed Nikko outside.

One by one, Nikko lifted the bundles out of the carriage, setting them on the ground. Some were small and light, like the white box that felt like it was full of air. Some were large and heavy, like the brown sack that came out last.

Nikko slung the sack over his shoulder. "This sugar goes to the kitchen," he told Anna. "Let's make that our first stop." He seemed happy to have a helper.

"This sugar will be good for baking, Anna," Olina said as Nikko hoisted the sack onto a shelf.

"But not right now," said Anna. "I have work to do!" She grinned. Now she was just as busy as the other people in the castle.

The next delivery was for Kai and Gerda. It was a feather duster. Anna dipped the feather duster as if it were her dance partner. Then she twirled with it all the way to the castle library, where Kai and Gerda were tidying the shelves.

Anna held the new delivery behind her back. "I have something for you," she said brightly.

"Is it my birthday?" Gerda asked.

"It's delivery time!" Anna exclaimed. It felt like she was giving Gerda a present.

Next Nikko brought a crate of onions for Anders, the gardener. Anna helped him load it onto a cart and roll it through the castle courtyard to the garden.

This delivery was mysterious, Anna thought. Didn't onions belong in the kitchen? But there were many things she did not know about life in the castle. Maybe onions were Anders's favorite food.

When Anna and Nikko found him, Anders was trimming a hedge. "We have your onions!" Anna announced.

Nikko and Anders both looked at her, confused. "Onions?" Anders asked.

"Yes," said Anna, opening the crate. "Enough to last a long time."

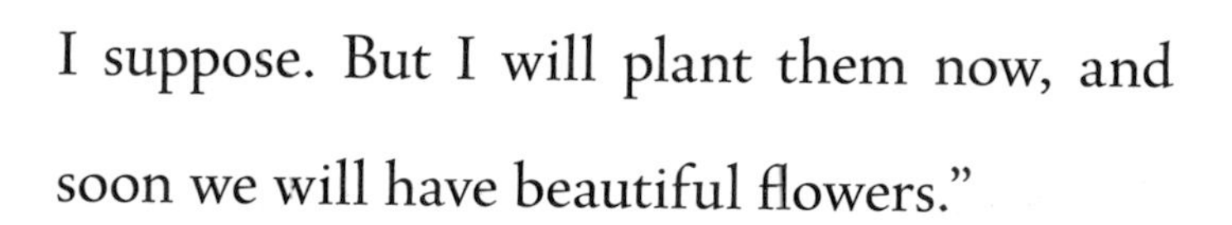

Anders peered into the crate and laughed. "Those are my tulip bulbs!" he said. "They do look like onions, I suppose. But I will plant them now, and soon we will have beautiful flowers."

Anna spent the rest of the morning following Nikko everywhere, from the bell tower to the guard tower and from the chapel to the Great Hall. Nikko did the heavy lifting, and Anna pushed his cart. Anna loved visiting every corner of the castle. She loved the way each of the bundles felt like a big surprise.

When they finished their work, Anna and Nikko returned to the kitchen, where Miss Larsen was waiting for them. Nikko put his feet up to rest, but Anna could not stay. Miss Larsen said, "It's time for your lessons, Anna. You will see Nikko again tomorrow."

Anna waved goodbye to Nikko as she followed her governess out of the kitchen. Making deliveries had almost made Anna forget missing her parents—and Elsa.

Chapter 3
A Friend and a Letter

The next day, Anna could hardly wait for Nikko to arrive. As she helped Olina bake a batch of sweet rolls, Anna listened for the jingle of his carriage.

Olina measured the milk and the yeast and let Anna add the flour to a big bowl. Anna did not like waiting for the dough to rise, but she liked the way it looked when it did. The dough was puffy now, like a pillow.

Carefully, Olina cut the dough into long strips. It was Anna's job to curl the strips of dough into spirals.

"Now we sprinkle a bit of sugar on top," Olina said. "And then we bake them!"

Anna coated her own spirals in a thick layer of sugar. These, she knew, would be especially delicious.

Anna heard the telltale jingle of Nikko's carriage just as Olina took the sweet rolls out of the big castle oven.

"He's here!" Anna cried out, rushing to the door.

Today Nikko had brought spices for the kitchen. "This cinnamon is just what these sweet rolls need," Olina said. She sprinkled cinnamon on all the rolls, making them smell delicious. When Anna took a bite, the cinnamon melted in her mouth.

As Anna ate, Nikko brought a pile of neatly folded cloth inside. Anna could see it had many different patterns and textures. Some pieces were smooth and shiny, like satin. Others looked soft and fuzzy. "Who will wear these?" Anna asked Nikko.

Laughing, Nikko said, "Well, no one will wear them yet. That is fabric for making clothes." Or costumes, Anna thought hopefully.

Nikko also brought tools and baskets

and buckets and papers. When a breeze blew through the open kitchen window, though, the papers scattered everywhere.

Anna dashed around the kitchen catching them, and then arranged them in a neat pile for Nikko. That's when she saw that the papers were envelopes with writing on them.

"What are these?" Anna asked.

"Those are some letters I brought for your parents," Nikko said. "Castle business, invitations, news. Letters are the way they stay connected with the world."

"Oh!" Anna said. Too bad none of them were for her. She would love to get a letter someday—an invitation, or some news from

far away. Maybe one day she would have someone to send letters to. How long would she have to wait until she could write her own letter?

And then she had an idea. What if she didn't wait at all?

When Nikko had left and her lessons were over, Anna returned to the portrait gallery. "Feeling braver?" she asked the girl on the swing. Anna, too, was about to try something she had never tried before. She was about to write a letter.

She picked up her favorite quill and dipped it in a pot of ink. Carefully, she decorated a plain piece of paper with drawings of flowers. Now it looked like the finest stationery in Arendelle.

There was only one problem. She did not know what to say.

Nikko had mentioned sending news, but Anna did not have any.

She tapped the end of her quill on the paper. She stood up and walked around the gallery. After a while, Anna decided to take a walk outside. Maybe it would give her a good idea.

Anna circled the garden and found where Anders had planted the bulbs. She walked by a tree that had just burst into bloom. As she stopped to smell a blossom on a low-hanging branch, Anna noticed something moving in the nearby hedge. She turned to see what it was, but the movement stopped when she turned.

Maybe she had just imagined it.

When she stepped around the garden fountain, though, she saw the movement again. Something was definitely there.

Anna froze. If she stayed in one spot, maybe whatever it was would forget she was there and go away. Then again, maybe it would come even closer. She was a little bit scared and a little bit curious all at once.

The castle gates were closed, so it probably wasn't a person. Could it be a mouse? A bird? A . . . monster? Anna hugged herself to stop from shivering.

Anna heard some rustling. Then she saw a ripple as whatever it was tunneled through the bushes and emerged on the castle walkway right in front of her!

A tiny red squirrel sat there, blinking, just as surprised as Anna.

Anna stood very still, because she did not want to scare him away.

The squirrel peered at her for a moment. Finally, he seemed to decide Anna was safe. He jumped across the walkway and into another patch of grass.

Anna watched as the squirrel disappeared into the shadow behind a flowerpot, then popped out on the other side. He raced by some lilies of the valley, then bounced into a bed of strawberry plants.

She lost sight of him for a little while. Then she noticed the squirrel between the rows of plants, helping himself to a treat. He held a strawberry in his tiny paws and nibbled with his tiny mouth.

"You are so cute," Anna told the squirrel. "Would you like another one?"

The squirrel scampered backward at the sound of her voice, but he did not run away.

Slowly, Anna reached beneath the leaves and pulled another strawberry off its stalk. She held it in both hands and reached toward the squirrel.

Would he dare to take the berry from her? Anna held her breath.

But this squirrel was not shy. He stood tall to reach her hand, then snatched the berry away. His tail twitched as he ate the berry in several bites, the way Anna might eat an apple.

They watched each other until the squirrel bounced away.

Anna was sorry to see him go, but now

she had the good idea she had been waiting for. She had something to write in her letter. She would write about the squirrel!

When Anna returned to the portrait room, she flopped down on the floor. Before she wrote anything, she drew a quick sketch and showed it to her friends in the paintings.

"Have you ever seen such a sweet squirrel?" she asked the girl on the swing.

"He'd be welcome at any picnic, right?" she asked the people on the blanket.

Maybe the squirrel, too, would become one of her friends.

Then Anna started to write.

"Dear Astrid," she began, making up someone to write to on the spot. "Wait till you hear this! I met someone new today. He is a squirrel, as red as a tulip and as friendly as a kitten. I do not know his name, or what he does when he is not in the garden. He disappeared before I could find out! I will be sure to let you know what happens next! Love, Anna." She signed her name with a flourish.

Writing about it was almost as exciting as meeting the squirrel in the first place,

Anna decided. She would write a letter every time she saw her new squirrel friend! Now her imagination was running wild. Each letter could be like a chapter in a book, she thought. Her squirrel story would have many parts and, Anna hoped, a happy ending.

Chapter 4
In the Treetop

Before Nikko arrived the next morning, Anna walked into the library, where Olina was arranging books. "Could you help me send a letter?" she asked.

"A letter for your parents? How lovely!" Olina said.

"Oh, no," Anna explained. "This is a letter for a friend."

Olina's eyes grew wide. "A friend?" she

asked. She knew Anna did not leave the castle or play with other children.

"Like my friends in the paintings," Anna explained. They were perfectly real to her.

"I see, I see," Olina replied, smiling.

She showed Anna how to fold her letter carefully and put it in an envelope. "Next, we write the address here," Olina instructed, pointing to the center of the letter. "Where does Astrid live?"

Anna made up an address just as quickly as she had made up Astrid. "Her address is One Pumpkin Pie, Across the Bridge and Over the Mountain, Kingdom of Arendelle," Anna announced. Some of the words were hard to spell, but Anna managed to squeeze them all onto the envelope.

"Now we just need to seal it!" Olina said.

Anna learned her parents used a special seal on all their letters. It was a round stamp that showed the crest of the kingdom, a crocus. As a member of the royal family, Anna could use the seal herself!

Olina led Anna out of the library to a pantry in the kitchen, where sticks of wax were stored alongside the candles.

"We will heat this wax until it is hot enough to melt," Olina explained.

She lit a match and held the flame to the very tip of a stick of wax. Before long, the top of the wax stick turned to liquid. It reminded Anna of the candles on her birthday cake.

Just as it looked ready to drip, Olina tilted the wax stick over Anna's letter. A tiny drop landed where Anna had closed the envelope!

"Quickly now," said Olina. From an

intricate wooden box, she took out a gold circle that bore the seal of the kingdom. Before the wax melted, Anna stamped it with the circle and left the imprint of the crocus.

Anna loved the way her letter seemed official now. No one would ever know it came from the younger princess. To anyone outside the castle, this could be a letter from the king or queen. Or from Elsa, Anna realized, since her older sister was the only other person who could use the seal. Thinking of her sister gave Anna a pang of sadness. Did Elsa write to other people, when she hardly spoke to Anna?

The sadness lifted as soon as Anna heard the familiar sound of Nikko's carriage coming to the kitchen door. She rushed outside the moment he stopped his horse. "I have a letter to send today!" she called to him, waving it in the air.

Nikko had just lifted a heavy wooden barrel from the back of his carriage, but he put it down to take the letter from Anna. "Looks very important," he noted, looking at the seal and reading the address. "I will make sure it gets to . . . One Pumpkin Pie." Nikko took a burlap bag from the front of the carriage and tucked the letter safely into its pocket.

Once Nikko left, Anna went to the schoolroom, but she had a hard time staying focused. Anna didn't want to memorize the names of past rulers or read maps when she could be outside. As soon as her lessons were done, Anna raced through the kitchen on her way to the garden. Would her new squirrel friend come out to play?

Olina, who was cleaning the counters, peered out into the afternoon fog. "It's a little drizzly out there," she told Anna.

But nothing could keep Anna from exploring the garden, not even a giant stack of pancakes with chocolate chips and whipped cream. She secured the hood of her jacket over her head and raced into the light rain.

It was not that different from snow, Anna thought. She stuck out her tongue to catch raindrops, just the way she and Elsa used to catch snowflakes in the winter. She found two acorns and placed them side by side in a small stream of water created by the rain. Which would float faster? she wondered. She also hoped they would catch the squirrel's eye.

Then, suddenly, the squirrel appeared! He darted out from under the hedge, leaves flying behind him. Anna was sure he was the same one, with his red fur and bright eyes. The squirrel took a few steps toward Anna and walked right into a puddle.

She thought he might take a swim in the puddle, or maybe a bath, but then he dipped his little face into the puddle and began to drink. When he finished, Anna could see tiny drops still clinging to his whiskers.

Was he ready to play with her now? Anna wondered.

He was—but not with her. The squirrel dashed through the flower garden, past the berry patch, and up a tree trunk!

Anna hurried to follow him. She loved

to climb trees! She jumped high to catch the tree's lowest branch, then pulled herself up so she was sitting. From there, she could climb the tree's branches like a ladder. It was hard to keep up with the squirrel, though. He scampered way up ahead of her, then paused.

Was he watching her climb? Anna wondered. Did he want her to follow him? Where was he going?

There was a big distance between Anna and the next branch, so it took her a moment to hoist herself up. But when she finally got balanced on the limb, the squirrel was gone.

Anna looked in every direction, but she

couldn't see her squirrel friend, no matter how hard she tried. He had disappeared into the leaves near the top of the tree, and Anna knew that a squirrel could easily jump from treetop to treetop. There was no telling where he was now.

She could be waiting a long time for him to come back, and Anna did not like to wait. She longed to have a playmate that afternoon. But at least she had a letter to write.

Chapter 5
A Surprise

"Dear Astrid," Anna wrote, back in the portrait gallery. Her clothes were still damp from the rainy weather, but she was too excited to change. "I saw the squirrel again today! He hasn't told me his name yet, so I have made one up for him. I have decided to call him Soren. Too bad he disappeared into the trees before we could play."

She paused to put more ink on her quill,

thinking. There had to be more to this story. Where did Soren live? What did he like to do? What was waiting for him, high above the garden?

Anna drew a picture of Soren in the tree, barely visible behind some bright green leaves, and continued writing. "I waited for him to come back, but he never did. Maybe his family lives in the treetops. I think they were calling him home."

She looked up at one of the large paintings on the wall. "Just a second, Joan," Anna said to the woman holding a sword and sitting on a white horse. Now her mind was racing. Did Soren have brothers and sisters? Did he have friends . . . or enemies? What other animals lived in the garden?

Anna decided she needed more details before she finished her letter, so she carefully folded what she had written and put it in her pocket to finish later.

The next morning, she was in the garden as soon as the castle's doors could be opened. Anna climbed tree after tree, looking up into the branches, until her hands were scraped. She cooled them off in the fountain, wiped them on her dress, and resumed her search.

Soren had been under the hedge the day before, she remembered. Anna swept away some leaves and crawled under the hedge herself. It was dark and quiet, and when Anna found a pile of pine needles, she wondered if it was a nest. Still, though, there was no sign of the squirrel.

Anna stood up and brushed herself off.

Maybe he would come back if he saw something interesting, she thought.

She strolled over to the edge of the garden, where the grass grew longer, and found a patch of cheery yellow flowers. Carefully, she picked a whole bunch of them, taking care that she did not break the stems. Then she settled herself on a sunny spot and wove the stems together until she had made a crown.

Who wouldn't be tempted by a crown of dandelions? It might be too big for Soren's head, Anna realized, but it would make a perfect toy for a squirrel.

Where was Soren?

Maybe he was off on an adventure, Anna thought. She tried to be happy for her friend.

But she wanted to be having an adventure, too. Right then Anna felt like she was playing some strange kind of hide-and-seek, where she was doing all the seeking and none of the hiding. All by herself.

Discouraged, Anna sighed and returned to the kitchen. Olina had poured a kettle of hot water into the sink as she prepared to wash some dishes, and her face was lost in a cloud of steam.

"Is everything all right?" Olina asked as the steam cleared away.

"No," admitted Anna. "Not really. I can't find Soren anywhere!"

Olina looked concerned. "Who is Soren?" she asked. Strangers were not allowed on castle property.

She should have mentioned Soren sooner, Anna realized. Olina could have helped her find him.

"He is an adorable red squirrel," Anna explained, "and I think he lives in the castle garden. I saw him wading in a puddle and I chased him up a tree, and then I made him a crown, but now he is gone. . . ."

When Anna finished, Olina sighed. She

was so quiet that Anna wondered if she had done something wrong. "What is it?" Anna asked. "Have you seen him?" Suddenly, she was worried about Soren. Was he hurt?

"No, no," Olina said, shaking her head. "I hope I do get to see him. I have never seen a red squirrel. It's just that sometimes I wish . . ."

She paused, and Anna wondered what Olina could wish.

"I just wish you had someone to play with," Olina finished.

Anna was surprised. She'd had no idea that the wish would have anything to do with *her*!

What would it be like to have a person to play with, though? Anna wondered. She imagined what she would do with that kind of friend. They could play tag in the garden. They could climb trees side by side. They could swim and skate and sing their favorite songs at the top of their lungs. It would be almost like having Elsa back, Anna thought. Soren was not quite that kind of friend.

Her thoughts were interrupted by the jingle that signaled Nikko's arrival.

"Nikko is my friend," Anna said brightly. "Let's go and see what he has for us today!"

Nikko's carriage was bursting with supplies. There was a new set of dishes, some ink for the royal inkwells, and even hay for the horses.

When he had finally finished his rounds, Nikko took out his burlap bag and turned to Anna. "I almost forgot!" he said. "Today I have a special delivery for you."

He took an envelope from the bag and handed it to Anna. She could hardly believe her eyes. Inside the envelope, there was a letter for her!

"Dear Anna," the letter said. "I am sorry to hear that your squirrel friend has gone. Perhaps he has taken a trip? Don't worry.

I know that you will see him again soon. Unless he has become invisible?"

There was a picture at the bottom. It was a sketch of a squirrel peeking out of a hole in a tree.

It was a wonderful picture, but Anna did not notice it at first because her eyes were searching the end of the letter. That was where the person who had written the letter would sign their name.

And the signature said, "Love, Astrid."

Chapter 6
Make Believe

Anna begged Nikko to stay while she wrote back. "I don't want Astrid to have to wait for my reply," she explained. She did not want to wait, either. The sooner she wrote to Astrid, the sooner she would get a letter back.

She raced up to her room and retrieved the letter she had been working on the night before. Anna loved Astrid's idea. An invisible squirrel! It gave her at least a dozen new ideas of her own.

"If Soren is invisible, that would explain a lot," Anna added to what she had written the night before. It was even more exciting to write now that she got to respond to someone else's words! "But I am not sure he knows how to disappear. What if he is learning to fly? Love, Anna."

Anna drew a picture of Soren flying between two birds, using his bushy tail to steady himself against the wind. If he were a flying squirrel, Anna thought, he could visit places around the world. Maybe he was traveling right now!

As Nikko waited, Anna folded the envelope, and Olina applied the royal seal. Anna admired it before she gave it to Nikko to deliver. She was proud to send something from the castle to her mysterious new friend.

The next day, she sat by the window for so long that there was a smudge where she

kept breathing on the glass. When Nikko's carriage finally crossed the bridge to the castle, Anna tore down the spiral stairs and through the kitchen door to meet him.

"Is there anything for me?" she asked, running to keep up with the carriage. "Is there a letter?"

Nikko drew his horse to a stop. He turned around and rummaged in his burlap bag. "Yes, I believe I do have something for you," he said. "Unless I left it behind. . . ."

The twinkle in his eye told Anna he was teasing. He broke into a smile as he handed her another envelope.

Nikko patted the bag. "I kept it right

here for safekeeping," he told Anna. "I knew it was something important."

Anna remembered to thank Nikko before she snatched the letter out of his hand. In her rush to see what was inside, she ripped the envelope open.

Like Anna, Astrid was still thinking about Soren. "Dear Anna," the letter said. "If Soren can fly, he is a very special squirrel. What else do you think he can do?"

Anna had been wondering about that herself! Soren could have powers that most squirrels only dreamed of. . . .

"Dear Astrid," she wrote back. "Sometimes I think he can speak in a language that we don't know. Or that maybe we can't hear."

She drew a picture of Soren playing with a pair of rabbits and a robin. "What if the animals can all talk to each other?" Anna asked Astrid. "What if they want to talk to people, but they don't know how?"

Anna had a new spring in her step after Nikko left with her latest letter. She would love to swim or skate or sing with a friend, it was true. But the best thing to do with a friend was play pretend.

Back when they were little, Anna and Elsa had pretended all the time. They imagined that they were polar bear sisters, or explorers in the snow, and those stories never ended. They just kept adding to them every time they played. Writing to Astrid reminded Anna of the best times with Elsa.

Anna did not quite understand how a person she had imagined—Astrid—had suddenly come to life. But there were plenty of things she did not understand, like why Elsa had stopped speaking to her, or why the sun rose and set, or why she did not like the taste of pickled herring. So Anna just accepted Astrid for who she was. And with Astrid to write to, it was hard for Anna to stop pretending.

In the morning, she set an extra place at the table for Astrid. "Who will be joining you for breakfast?" Olina asked.

"A friend," Anna said.

"The squirrel?" Olina replied. "I do not think that is a good idea."

Anna's laugh rang through the grand dining room. "No, silly," she corrected Olina. "Astrid!" Mealtime was lonely without her parents, but Astrid could keep Anna company. At least in her imagination.

During her lessons, Anna was distracted. "Your head is in the clouds," Miss Larsen said, but that only made Anna think about

clouds. Could Soren fly that high? She would have to ask Astrid what she thought of that.

Anna wandered the garden, looking for butterflies, before Nikko was due with his carriage. She didn't see any fluttering wings, but she did spot a scampering squirrel just when she least expected him.

"Soren!" said Anna. He backed away from her voice, but he did not run away. He cocked his head a little, like he was saying hello, then hopped over to the willow tree.

If he climbed, Anna thought, she would keep up with him this time. Instead, Soren began digging a small hole in the dirt.

Was he digging for fun? Anna wondered. The way she and Elsa used to play in the sand? Or was he after buried treasure? Anna had imagined a whole pirate ship and a trunk of gold coins before she realized that what Soren had dug up was a treasure only a squirrel could love: a stash of acorns.

Soren stuffed two of them in his mouth and scurried away. He was halfway across the garden when Anna realized he had left one behind. "Come back!" she called, but he had vanished beneath the hedge.

Anna picked up the acorn and turned it over in her hand. Had Soren left the acorn for her on purpose? Anna liked to think so. Luckily, she knew just whom to give it to.

My Favorite Things:
-Chocolate
-Reindeer
- Home
-Winter

Chapter 7
A Visitor

That night, Anna sat down at the desk in her bedroom. She began a letter to Astrid at once, tucking Soren's acorn into the envelope. "Look what Soren was hiding!" Anna wrote. "I wonder what other treasures he has buried."

Astrid, like Anna, loved the idea that Soren was keeping secrets. Her next letter said, "Make sure you look for his treasure map. You never know where it could lead you. Maybe to the end of a rainbow?"

She had drawn a picture of a rainbow and enclosed a gift of her own for Anna. "I will save the acorn from Soren's collection, and I am sending a stone from my own collection for you to keep."

Anna looked carefully at the stone, as if it could tell her more about Astrid. It was small and round, and as smooth as glass. If she looked closely, she could almost see through it. The stone was brilliant, like a jewel. Was it an opal? Anna wondered. A

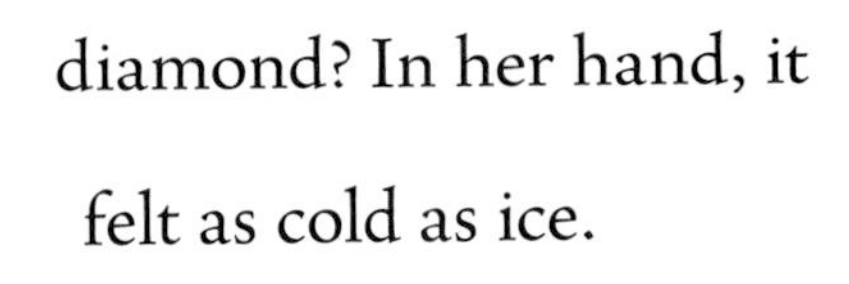

diamond? In her hand, it felt as cold as ice.

Ice reminded Anna of her sister and all the fun they used to have in winter. But she was not sure she wanted to tell Astrid about Elsa. Astrid was good at pretending, but Anna's feelings were *real*.

What was Astrid even like? Anna wondered. She didn't know yet, but they could get to know each other through letters. Maybe someday she could visit!

Anna knew that sometimes she asked too many questions, and she did not want

Astrid to get tired of writing! Instead of asking Astrid anything, Anna decided, first she would tell Astrid about herself. If she started this conversation, maybe Astrid would join in.

Anna picked up another piece of paper and wrote in big letters across the top, "My favorite things." Then she listed some of the things she loved.

"I could eat chocolate for every meal," Anna wrote. "Yes, even for breakfast. Chocolate is my favorite food."

She loved squirrels, of course. But they were not her very *favorite* animal. "My favorite animals are reindeer," she wrote to

Astrid. "Someday I hope I get the chance to ride one!"

Anna did not even know where Astrid lived. "I live near the mountains, on a sparkling fjord," she added. "My favorite place is home."

When Astrid's reply came, Anna opened it so quickly that the envelope fell to the floor. The letter was all Anna had hoped for and more. "I love chocolate, too!" Astrid wrote. "And if you can believe it, I also live in the mountains. My favorite game is hide-and-seek." Just like Anna's!

Anna could hardly believe her eyes. "What is your favorite season?" she wrote.

"Mine is winter. I love snow angels, sleds, and snowballs."

Once again, the girls agreed. "I love ice-skating under the stars," Astrid wrote. "And warming up by a hot fire."

"Do you have any brothers or sisters?" Anna dared to write.

"I have a little sister," Astrid said. "There's no one I'd rather play with."

Anna stood up, stretched her arms, and walked around her room. She was writing at least one letter a day by now, and maybe it was time to take a break. There was plenty of time to finish her reply before Nikko arrived again.

Astrid had helped the first week of Anna's parents' trip go by quickly. While Anna still missed her mom and dad, it was nice writing with Astrid.

Anna opened her bedroom door and walked out into the quiet hallway. As she passed Elsa's room, she put an ear to the door, but she did not hear a sound. With their parents away, Anna had only seen Elsa open her door when Olina delivered meals, but the rest of the time the door was shut tight. What did she do? Anna wondered. Usually, their mother and father spent some time with Elsa, but since they were gone, she must have been alone all day. At least Anna had Astrid to write to while they were gone. Did Elsa ever get lonely, too?

As she descended the staircase, Anna could hear pots and pans in the kitchen, where Olina was making dinner. She could see Kai and Gerda shining the floors in the Great Hall.

This was the time of day when Anna would settle in to read stories with her father. She would meet him in the council chambers, where he was happy to step away from his royal duties. Anna loved the way he gave different voices to all the characters in a book. Her father knew how to make a story come to life! Today, though, Anna slipped into the library to read on her own.

The library had two tall bookcases stretching from the floor to the ceiling and a great stone fireplace to keep the room cozy. There wasn't a fire this evening, but Anna didn't mind. She curled up in a chair in the middle of the room, ready to get lost in a book. If she couldn't go on an adventure, Anna liked to read about adventures.

But there was a rattling in the chimney, and Anna couldn't concentrate. Then there was a clunk, like something falling.

Nothing had sparked a fire, but the sounds sparked Anna's imagination. Could there be a ghost in the library? she wondered. Anna had never considered that before, but there were plenty of ghost stories on the shelves.

Then she had a burst of understanding. It had to be Astrid, coming for a visit! She had never been to the castle, so she couldn't find the door. Silly Astrid, coming down the chimney.

When she got up to look for herself, Anna could see that she was right and wrong. It was a visitor at the wrong entrance, yes. But it wasn't Astrid. It was Soren!

He was covered in soot from the chimney, but he didn't seem hurt, just surprised. His eyes darted to every corner of the library. "Did you climb a tree and follow it to the roof?" Anna asked. "Did you take your exploring a little bit too far? Or are you a king, looking for a castle?"

Thinking quickly, Anna ran to her room and came back with an empty jewelry box. She put the box down on the ground and waited patiently to see what the squirrel would do. Soren, as if he knew Anna's plan, cautiously sniffed around the box before hopping inside. Anna smiled and carefully picked up the jewelry box to take it and

Soren outside. Squirrels didn't belong inside, she knew, and she would have to return him to the garden. But Soren's visit gave her a brilliant idea!

Chapter 8

A Castle for the King

Not that long ago, Anna had loved to build things with Elsa, and Anna had a feeling that Astrid would be a good builder, too. Building was a sort of make believe, after all, and Anna knew that Astrid loved to pretend. That was one reason they were friends!

"Dear Astrid," Anna wrote the following day. "Soren came to visit me last night, and

I discovered something we did not know before. Soren is the king of all squirrels! He lives under the hedge right now, but I think he really wants to live in a castle. Would you like to help me make a castle for the king?"

Astrid's next letter exclaimed "YES!" in capital letters. "How do we get started?"

Anna had already thought about this. She would start building, then draw pictures to show Astrid her work. Then Astrid could make suggestions after looking at the pictures. That way, both of their ideas would be included.

"It is a little tricky because we are not

together," Anna wrote. "But I think that we can do it."

That afternoon, Anna went to the gardens to gather sticks and leaves for building. When Soren spotted her, he twitched his nose and rolled in a patch of moss. Anna thought maybe he was grateful she had rescued him, and she wanted to stop to play. But she had too many things to do!

First she had to find the perfect place for the castle. Soren loved the garden, but he also liked the privacy of the hedge. Anna walked around the garden several times until she found a shady spot under the willow tree. It was protected by the willow branches, but it was close to everything else Soren loved—even his acorns.

Anna started building the castle by placing a line of sticks on the ground. Then, very carefully, she stacked the sticks into four walls, filling in the gaps with leaves and berries. She thought the berries were a colorful touch until King Soren darted toward the walls of his castle and ate them!

Maybe there was a reason that people did not make castles out of food they liked to eat, Anna thought. Imagine if her castle were made of chocolate! Anna removed the remaining berries from the wall and

left them in a pile for the squirrel. Then she substituted pine needles for the berries, pressing them between the sticks until all the walls were the same shape and size.

After the first day of building, Anna went to the portrait room to draw pictures for Astrid. "Castles can take years to build," Anna wrote beside her sketches. "But I think we have made a good start."

Before she left the portrait room, Anna apologized to her friends in the paintings. "I'm sorry I haven't visited in a while," she said. She hoped they would understand why she was playing with her new friend. They had one another for company, after all. But she would come back to visit them often, since she knew how it felt to get left behind.

Astrid's next letter was packed with great ideas for the castle. "What if we make separate rooms inside?" she wrote. "I think Soren needs a playroom, don't you?"

Anna could not believe she had not thought of that herself! As soon as she put down Astrid's letter, she ran outside to build some pebble walls inside the castle, dividing Soren's bedroom from his playroom. She filled the playroom with pine cones for toys. Even kings needed to play, she decided.

Soren might not need a

kitchen, but Anna blocked off a corner of the house for storage. Maybe he did not want to bury *all* his acorns.

"It is perfect!" Astrid wrote back. "Do you think we should build him a bed?"

Anna found a piece of moss for Soren to rest on, and some leaves for his blankets. What if he grew thirsty in the night? she wondered. That afternoon, Miss Larsen helped Anna make a bowl out of clay. Anna filled it with water and left it by Soren's nest.

After many letters, Astrid wrote, "I can't think of anything else to add," and Anna knew it was time to build the castle's roof.

She collected twigs and crisscrossed them on top of the castle. Then she tied them to the sides of the house with stalks and stems, and weighed them down with rocks. To make sure the castle could withstand storms, Anna shook it gently. But the castle remained strong. The castle was fit for a king.

Anna couldn't wait to show her parents what she and Astrid had built. They would be back in only a few days, and even though Anna now had Astrid and Soren to keep her company, Anna would be happy to see them.

Later that morning, Anna wrote another

letter in the library, then sat in the chair by the fireplace. She didn't mean to stay for long, but building a castle was hard work. Now they just needed Soren to move in, Anna thought as she drifted off to sleep. She and Astrid had been a great team. She loved feeling like part of a team again.

By the time her nap was over, Anna had missed Nikko and his deliveries, but Olina had left an envelope for Anna on a small table at the bottom of the stairs. Usually Anna tore the letters open so fast that she didn't even notice the envelopes, but this time something caught her eye. There was something strange on this envelope. Had it been on the others, all along?

It was the royal seal.

Chapter 9
Secret Mission

Anna blinked. That did not make any sense. How could Astrid's letter have *her* royal seal?

She took a closer look, but there was no mistake: it was the exact same seal, with the crocus in the middle.

How had Astrid gotten it? Anna wondered. She knew that the seal never left the castle.

Did that mean Astrid was *inside* the castle? Surely someone would have noticed an extra little girl.

Anna sat on the bottom step and tried to think of reasons Astrid could have the royal seal. Then Anna remembered what Olina had said. She had wished Anna had someone to play with.

Had Olina made up Astrid for Anna to have a friend? Or at least to write with? The realization that Astrid could have been Olina all along made Anna frown. If someone was pretending to be Astrid, that meant there wasn't a *real* Astrid. Anna was not part of a good team after all. Olina might have

meant to be nice, but now Anna was sadder than ever.

She found Olina sweeping the grand hall. Olina looked up and smiled when Anna walked in, but Anna did not smile back.

She waved the letter in the air. "Did you write this?" Anna asked.

"No, it's from Nikko," Olina said, looking surprised. "Well, really from your friend Astrid."

"That's what I thought, too," said Anna. She looked at the letter, her eyes filling with tears. "But now I know it can't be from Astrid. It has to be from someone inside the castle. Someone who can use our royal seal."

Olina stopped sweeping and bent down to Anna. She looked like she was debating her next words. "I promise I didn't write the letter, Anna," she finally said. She wiped away Anna's tears with her thumb, offering a kind smile. "Why don't you come with me to the kitchen? We can finish decorating some cookies before bed."

Anna gave one last sniff and followed Olina to the kitchen. She trusted Olina. If she said she hadn't written the letter, Anna believed her.

But as Anna helped Olina put sprinkles on a fresh batch of cookies, she couldn't stop thinking about the letter. Someone inside the castle had written it, and Anna was determined to catch that person in the act. That's why she was going to keep an eye on everyone in the castle.

The next day, Anna put on some soft shoes that were quiet when she walked and tiptoed through the castle halls.

She hid behind the doorframe while Kai and Gerda cleaned the windows in the council chambers. There were plenty of pens and paper in there, Anna noticed. The king had a desk in the council chambers for his official correspondence. It would be easy for Kai or Gerda to write letters on the sly.

But Kai and Gerda did not go near the

desk. They cleaned the floor till it was shining, and then they went to the king and queen's bedroom, preparing everything for their arrival home. Anna moved on, since they did not seem to be up to anything suspicious.

She kept an eye on Miss Larsen during

their lessons, but quickly decided her governess couldn't be behind the letters. As she wrote notes on the chalkboard, Anna realized Miss Larsen's handwriting looked nothing like Astrid's.

Could Nikko be the mystery writer? Anna followed him, keeping to the castle's shadows, when he made his next deliveries. He carried sacks and barrels and bags of supplies. He stopped to talk to the people in the castle workshop and in the stables. Anna could not hear what he was saying, but he was not acting unusual. He was cheerful and friendly, like always.

When Olina called Nikko into the kitchen, Anna watched from under a table. Nikko took a piece of paper from his pocket, and Anna drew in a breath. Was she about to catch him? But Nikko was not writing a letter. He was making a list of supplies to bring the next day.

Anna slipped out to the garden next. Anders, the gardener, was gathering fresh flowers. Anna tiptoed into his shed to see if there was any clue that he'd been writing letters from Astrid. Next to his seedlings, she saw a pile of blankets. Did he nap there when no one was watching?

Did that mean he was sneaky? Anna wondered. Or did it just mean he was tired?

Anna went to the portrait gallery when she got tired of spying. "Hello!" she said to her friends in the paintings, trying to sound cheerful. "I've missed you!"

She told them about Soren and his castle and Astrid and the letters. "Can you believe that someone was pretending to be someone they were not?" Anna asked them. It made her feel better to talk to them, but it wasn't quite the same as a real conversation. Anna wished she could write to Astrid.

Astrid's stone was in her pocket and

still as cold as ice. Anna took it out and gazed deeply into it, rubbing its cloudy surface. The stone was almost clear, and Anna wished she could see to its center, but the center remained as mysterious as Astrid's letters.

When Anna wandered back into the castle kitchen, Olina wasn't there.

Where could she be? Anna wondered.

She tiptoed into the Great Hall just in time to see Olina disappearing upstairs. Was she slipping away to use the royal seal?

Anna's heart was racing. Finally, she would have some answers!

Anna approached the stairs. She heard a door open, and Olina's soft voice. There was a pause, and then the door shut again.

Then she heard the sound of Olina's first step at the top of the stairs, heading down. When Anna spotted her, Olina was carrying an empty tray.

Anna shrank into a corner. She did not want Olina to see her spying.

Just as she did every day, Olina had delivered food on a tray to Elsa. Nothing unusual at all.

Anna stayed out of sight until she was sure Olina had passed by.

The Great Hall was so quiet that Olina's footsteps echoed against the floor.

It was lonely in the corner by herself, Anna thought. Just like it was lonely in the castle. Whoever she really was, Astrid—or the idea of Astrid—had helped keep Anna happy while her parents were away. Anna had written many letters and invented many stories. She had even built a castle! Now there was only one day left until her parents came home, and the time had flown by.

When she was thinking of her parents,

Anna's eyes darted in the direction of Elsa's door. What was her sister doing in there?

Elsa did not meet the day's deliveries or explore the gardens. She did not dance in her favorite dress, or talk to the paintings, or play hide-and-seek.

Was Elsa just as lonely as she was?

Astrid had helped Anna get to the end of her parents' long trip, whether or not she was real.

Was there a way for Anna to help Elsa, too?

Chapter 10
A Special Story

Anna did not like the feeling of losing a friend. But she still had one important friend left, and he was the one who had brought her and Astrid together in the first place!

Anna thought maybe he could help her make her sister smile.

The next day, she ran out to the gardens, then tiptoed toward Soren's house. If he was home, she did not want to wake him. Gingerly, she lifted the twigs off his roof and peeked in. There he was, curled up on his bed of moss!

Lifting out his tiny water bowl, Anna refilled it from the fountain. Then she reached her finger in to touch him gently. She had never really petted Soren before! His fur was as soft as goose down. His whiskers quivered as he slept. Was he romping with other squirrels in his dreams? Anna wondered.

Anna stepped away for a minute to brush pine needles off his front walkway. When she looked back in, Soren was awake!

He watched her intently, then leaped out of his bed. He did not use the door that Anna and Astrid had designed. Instead, Soren crawled out through his window!

Once he was out of his house, Anna had a hard time keeping up with Soren. He jumped over a patch of mint and ran through a pile of mulch. He scurried up one tree and down another, he rolled through a patch of wet grass, and he gobbled up one of Anders's flower bulbs before Anna could stop him.

Soren was full of energy! But that was exactly why Anna had decided to write some more about him. She would write down every detail.

Her first letters to Astrid had been a story, she remembered. It was the story of Soren!

But Anna had never finished writing that story, because she and Astrid had started writing about other things. They became friends when they started writing about their favorite things. They became friends when they shared their ideas.

Maybe Anna needed to let go of all the questions she still had about Astrid. She might never know the answers. All she knew was that Astrid, whoever she was, had been a great friend when Anna needed one, and now Anna could be a great friend to someone else. Even if that person was, well, more than just a friend. She was Anna's sister!

Anna was going to finish Soren's story now. She wasn't writing letters this time, though. She was going to write a book!

After following Soren around the garden, Anna trimmed some pieces of paper until they were as small as cards. She made a hole in each piece, then picked some long grasses from the edge of the garden. Carefully, she wove the grass through the pieces of paper to bind the pages of the book together. After that, she finally started to write.

"Once upon a time, there was a small squirrel in a big garden," Anna wrote. "He was as soft as a flower petal and as fast as a horse. And every day he had a new adventure."

Anna wrote about the trees he climbed and the berries he stole and the forest friends who would visit him in his new house. Some of it was true, and some of it was made up, but Anna knew something important now. Sometimes the memories that were made up felt just as real as the real memories. After all, that was certainly true of Astrid.

When Anna was finished, she read the whole story out loud to herself, and then she drew the pictures. They were so beautiful that even her friends in the paintings would be proud of them, Anna thought.

Since it was not a letter, it did not need an envelope or a seal. Anna wrote her own name in big letters on the book's cover, though, because she wanted anyone who happened to see it to know exactly who the author was.

Now she just needed to deliver it. There was no need to wait for Nikko this time. His deliveries came from far away, outside the castle, but this delivery was only going from downstairs to upstairs. So Anna waited until it was time for Olina to take up Elsa's dinner tray. "Can I carry it?" Anna asked before they went up.

Olina thought for a second. "I don't see why not," she said. "But you know you must not go into Elsa's room."

"I'll just carry the tray," Anna said. "You can be the one to bring it in."

Olina nodded. "Thank you for offering!" she said. "I can always use an extra pair of hands."

Olina spooned some hot stew into a bowl for Elsa and put some fresh rolls on a plate. When everything was ready, she put the tray into Anna's hands. "Careful, now," she warned. "Take it slow."

Anna held the tray steady all the way to the top of the stairs. Then, as Olina opened Elsa's door to walk in, Anna slipped her book under Elsa's napkin. It would be the first thing Elsa saw when she sat down to

eat, but Olina would never even know it was there.

There was only one problem. How would Anna know if Elsa liked it? She needed to stay upstairs a little longer.

"Can you take the tray down?" she asked Olina. "I need to get something from my room."

"Of course," said Olina.

Anna went to her room and waited a moment. Then she walked slowly past Elsa's room. Was that the sound of a page turning? Anna wondered, putting an ear to the door. Was that the sound of her sister's laugh?

As she strained to hear it, another sound rang out in the Great Hall.

It was the sound of her parents coming through the front door! With eager steps, Anna raced to welcome them home.

What she did not see as she hurried down the stairs, though, was another piece of paper, slipped out from under Elsa's door.

It was a letter, ready for Nikko to deliver another day. And fastened with the royal seal.

DON'T MISS THE FIRST BOOK IN THE SERIES!

Mulan's
SECRET PLAN

TURN THE PAGE FOR A SNEAK PEEK. . . .

Chapter 1

A Little Excitement

On the first day of school, Mulan woke up before the sun. This was not unusual, as Mulan always rose before dawn—she had to in order to complete her chores before breakfast. But this morning felt different. Today she was full of energy, as if everything in front of her were a challenge she couldn't wait to conquer. She wasn't just finishing chores before the sun rose—she was *racing* the sun, determined to move faster than the light could streak through the sky.

Mulan fed Little Brother, who barked in appreciation. "I'll have all sorts of stories to tell you later," she told her dog. In the chicken coop, Mulan scattered feed on the ground, dreaming about what the day might have in store: would she learn math today? Writing? She gathered up eggs from the coop: *one*,

two, *three*, she counted as the hens waddled toward their breakfast. She balanced the eggs carefully in her arms as she ran back toward her house, across the moon bridge, and over the pond.

Mulan skipped over the last few garden stones and leaped up the steps of her house into the kitchen, almost tripping over Little Brother. One of the eggs flew out from where she was clutching it against her robe, but she swooped down and caught it with her left hand before it cracked on the ground.

To be continued . . .